RUSHMORE

SCHOLASTIC PRESS ◆ NEW YORK

RUSHMORE

LYNN CURLEE

"Let us place there, carved high,

as close to heaven as we can . . . their faces,

to show posterity what manner of men they were.

Then breathe a prayer that these records

will endure until the wind and the rain alone

shall wear them away."

— GUTZON BORGLUM

JULY 4, 1930

THE MOUNTAIN IS A BARE, MASSIVE OUTCROPPING OF SOLID GRANITE. Ancient and very dense, the stone was formed deep within the earth as a great upwelling of hot molten rock slowly cooled and crystallized. Over eons, as the land rose to form mountains, the softer rock above and around it gradually eroded away until it was exposed about sixty million years ago. Now jutting from a pine-covered ridge on the flank of Harney Peak in the rugged and scenic Black Hills of South Dakota, it stands nearly six thousand feet above sea level, a blocky, irregular, flat-topped crag about one thousand feet long and four hundred feet wide. The vertical slab of its southeastern face forms a cliff three hundred feet high. On a crisp, clear morning in 1885, a young lawyer from New York gazed across the valley toward that spectacular cliff, furrowed, cracked, darkened, and stained by 600,000 centuries of weather. Charles E. Rushmore was visiting the Black Hills for his company, which owned tin mines in these ore-rich mountains. "What is its name?" he asked. Bill Challis, a local prospector and guide, answered, "Never had any, but it has now — we'll call her Rushmore."

Fifty-six years later, obscure Mount Rushmore had been transformed by a great artistic and engineering project into an important American patriotic shrine and tourist attraction.

For there, in the years between 1927 and 1941, four gigantic faces were blasted, drilled, and carved into the ancient cliff. Mount Rushmore National Memorial is the world's most colossal stone carving, and it is meant to celebrate the basic principles and highest ideals of American society. The faces are those of four important presidents of the United States — George Washington, Thomas Jefferson, Abraham Lincoln, and Theodore Roosevelt — men whose achievements represent the founding, expansion, preservation, and conservation of America. Its creators called the monument "The Shrine Of Democracy." Carved with great sensitivity and nobility of spirit in spite of their monumental scale, the four faces seem to emerge from the living rock and gaze serenely out over the American landscape into infinity.

◆ ◆ ◆

SOUTH DAKOTA

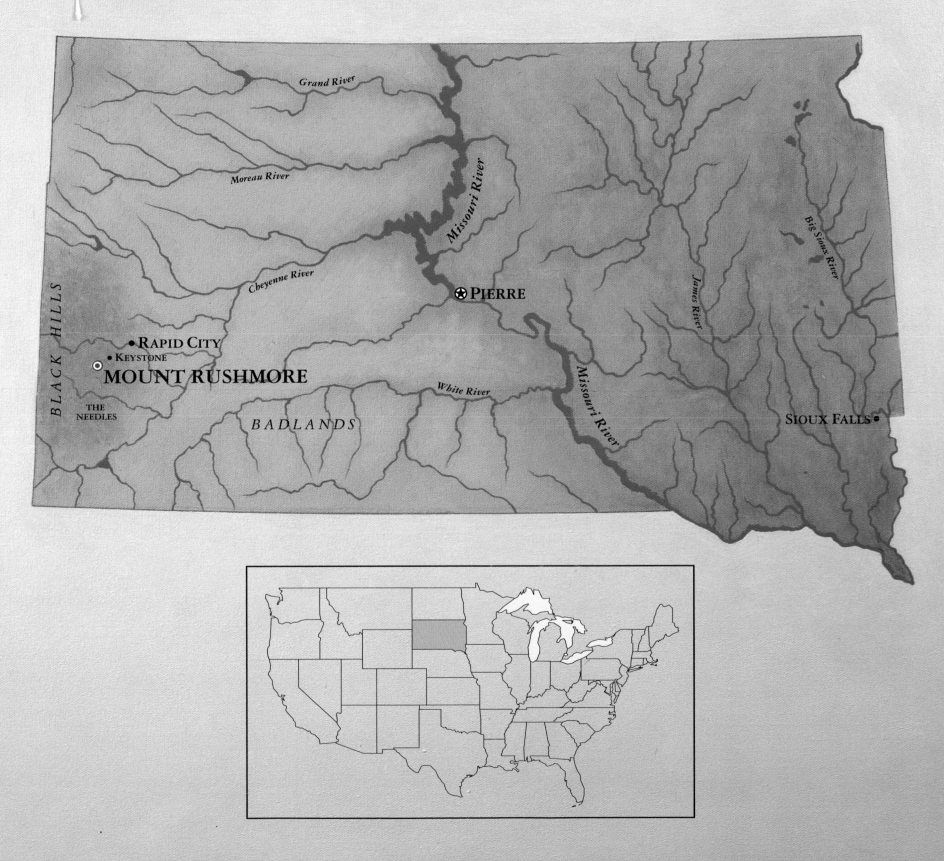

THE 1920S WERE A MONUMENTAL ERA. The events of the First World War had turned the United States into a world power. There was peace and prosperity, and the future seemed limitless. American industry was growing, great skyscrapers were being built in the large cities, and the automobile was transforming American life. It was Doane Robinson, state historian of South Dakota, who first had the idea of carving figures in the Black Hills. He proposed that figures from the Old West be carved into a group of granite spires called the "Needles." Besides serving as a tribute to the history of the state, which was only one generation removed from the frontier, Robinson argued that large statues would attract tourists, who were beginning to travel about the country in their newfangled automobiles. For most Americans in the 1920s, South Dakota was a fairly remote place.

Robinson began to present his idea, locally to businessmen and politicians, and nationally to several prominent sculptors. First he enlisted the support of Peter Norbeck, United States senator from South Dakota. A former governor and the state's most powerful politician, Senator Norbeck was particularly interested in the conservation and management of forests and wildlife. He was a leader in the national movement to preserve areas of great natural beauty and to make them accessible to the public by building scenic roads. His support was crucial. With his political savvy and network of friends and contacts, Senator Norbeck knew how to get things done. He instantly saw "wonderful possibilities in the proposition if it should fall into the hands of an artist big enough to handle it." But, as Robinson said, "the fellow who does it must be something more than a stone carver."

HIS FULL NAME WAS JOHN GUTZON DE LA MOTHE BORGLUM, and he was much more than a stone carver. He was a professional sculptor of some fame, with great talent and charm, a huge ego, and almost boundless ambition. Borglum was known for thinking, dreaming, and talking big, and in August 1924, at the age of fifty-seven, he was already carving a mountain when he received Doane Robinson's letter:

> *Mr. Gutzon Borglum*
> *Stone Mountain, Georgia*
>
> *Dear Mr. Borglum:*
> *In the vicinity of Harney Peak in the Black Hills*
> *of South Dakota are opportunities for heroic sculpture*
> *of unusual character. Would it be possible for you to*
> *design and supervise a massive sculpture there?*

Of course it was possible. It was just the opportunity Borglum had been hoping for. Within a month, he was in South Dakota to look things over. Solid and stocky, bald and

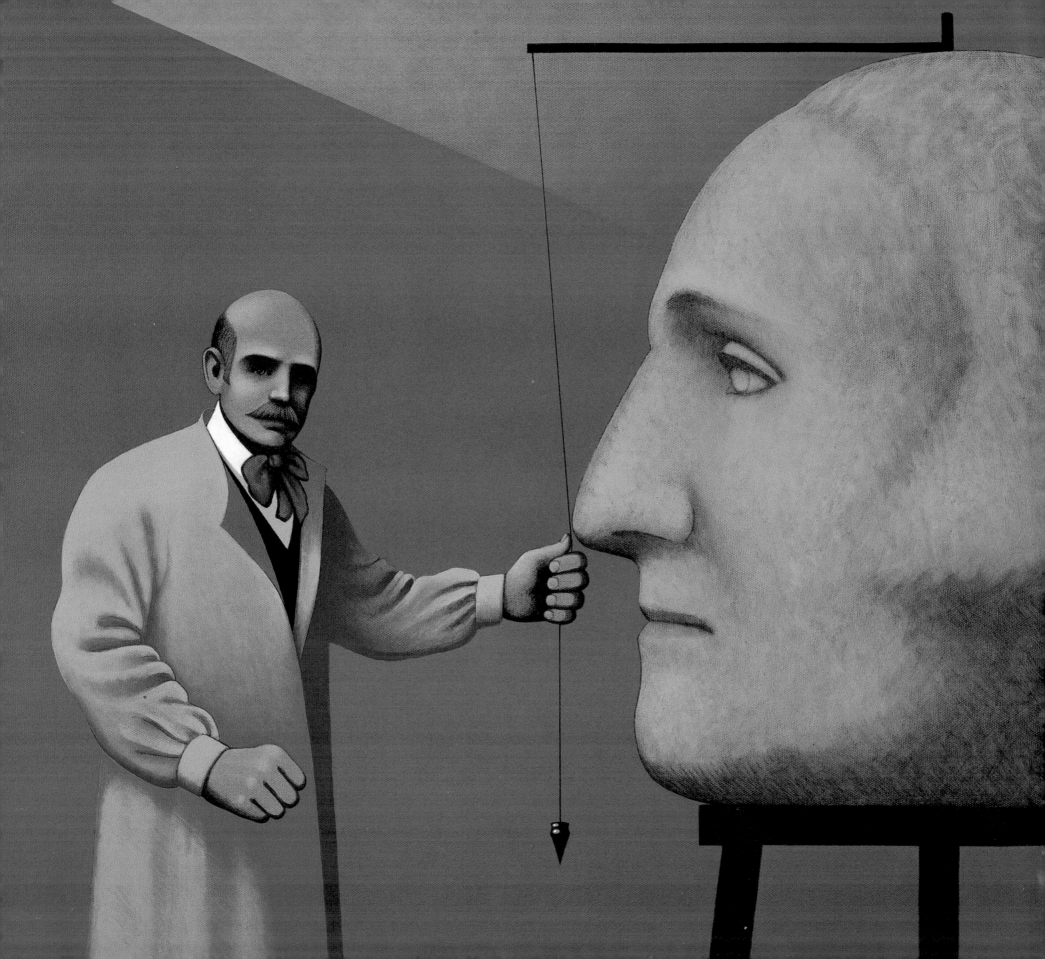

moustached, he was vivid and intense, with a commanding personality and strong opinions. He was interested in everything, considered himself an expert in many fields, and radiated enthusiasm and energy. Robinson and Norbeck had found their artist.

Born in 1867 in Idaho of Danish immigrants, Gutzon Borglum grew up in Fremont, Nebraska, a rough frontier town. At the age of sixteen, Gutzon made his way to San Francisco. He wanted to become a painter. By 1890, the young artist was married and living in Paris, where he studied and exhibited. The Borglums moved frequently, from Paris to California to London and back to Paris. During these years Borglum worked hard to refine his natural talent, and gradually the country boy from the Wild West became a successful artist and a worldly, sophisticated man. But he was restless. His marriage in trouble, homesick for America, Borglum was also at an artistic crossroads. He decided to give up painting. In 1901 he parted from his wife, returned to America, remarried, and settled in New York to pursue a new career as a sculptor.

During the next twenty years, Borglum established himself as a major American sculptor, executing many public and private commissions, and making a handsome living. Borglum believed in an American Art, with American subjects, presented simply, directly, and realistically, but with grandeur, and on an epic scale — an art to ennoble and inspire patriotic longings. Gutzon Borglum wanted to carve mountains, and at Stone Mountain he got his chance.

STONE MOUNTAIN IN GEORGIA IS A VAST GRANITE MONOLITH which emerges abruptly from the earth near Atlanta. For several years Borglum had been engaged in carving a monument to the heroes of the Confederacy on the flank of the massive rock. In January 1924, the head of General Robert E. Lee, the central figure, was unveiled with much publicity. It was the first of what were to be hundreds of figures in Borglum's grand plan. But by the time of his first visit to South Dakota later in the year, the Stone Mountain project was faltering. Gutzon Borglum was autocratic and domineering. *He* would be in control of *his* sculpture. On the other hand, the aristocratic Atlantans who considered Stone Mountain their project treated Borglum as an employee — an impossible situation for the headstrong artist. In 1925, he destroyed his working models and abandoned the job rather than submit to interference with his ideas. Accused of "offensive egotism and delusions of grandeur," Borglum retorted: "I destroyed the models for the greatest piece of sculpture in the world's history because I believe in the right of the artist to his own creation. I am ready to rot in jail before I concede this principle." Stone Mountain was placed in the hands of another artist.

But by now Borglum was convinced of his ability to carve mountains, and he needed to salvage his reputation and his bruised ego. The South Dakota proposal had gripped his imagination, and he decided to make it happen.

Borglum first saw Mount Rushmore during his second trip to South Dakota, in August 1925. The first visit the year before had gone very well. Borglum quickly convinced

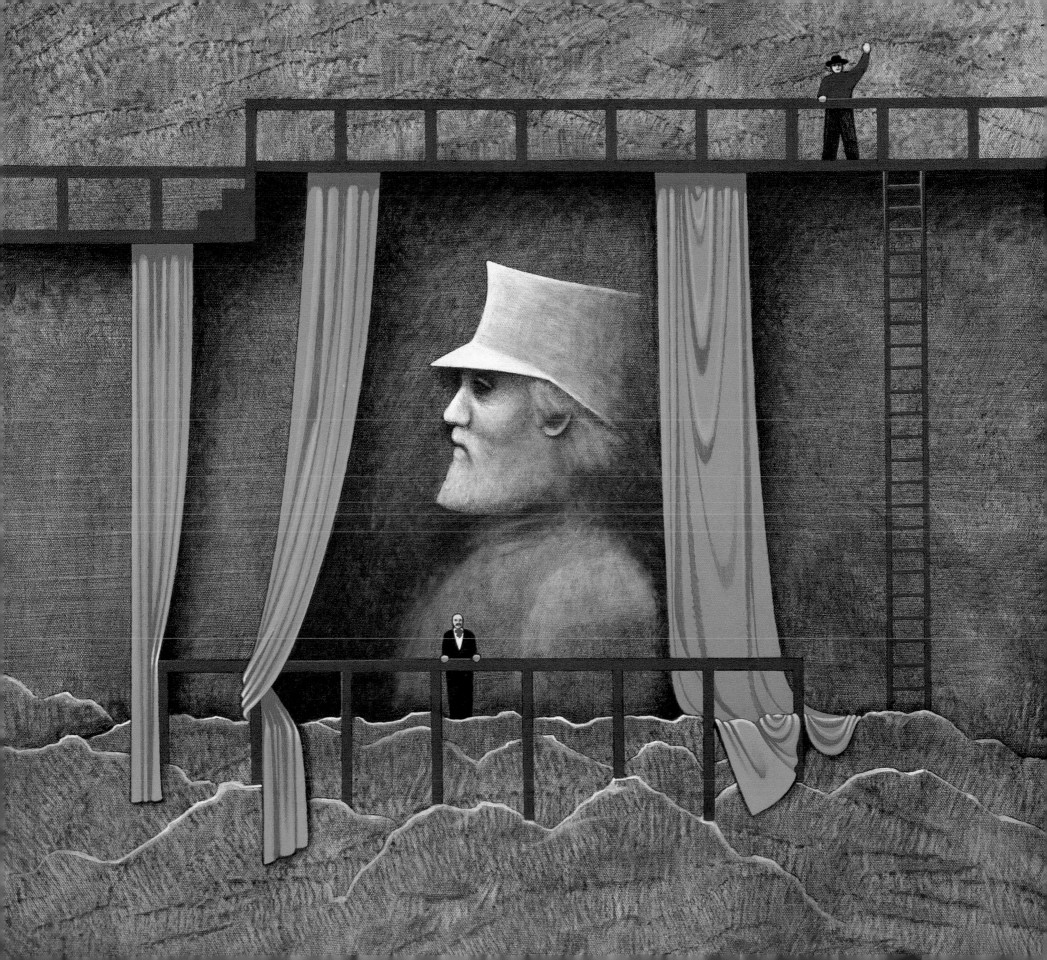

Robinson that the carvings should honor the greatest men in American history rather than figures from the Old West. He even sent a sketch of George Washington and Abraham Lincoln carved into the spires of the Needles. For his part, Senator Norbeck got legislation passed to allow carving in the Black Hills, parts of which are protected in a national forest. But the idea of tampering with these beautiful formations met with a great deal of opposition. "Man makes statues but God made the Needles. Let them alone," wrote one critic. A less controversial site had to be found. Borglum was shown several other rock formations in the Black Hills. Mount Rushmore was the most impressive. The rock seemed to be of the right quality for carving, it was beautifully lit by the sun, and it was large enough for Borglum's growing plans.

Senator Norbeck expressed concern about the lack of roads near Rushmore, but conceded that it was the best choice. Borglum quickly organized an elaborate dedication ceremony for October 1, 1925. There were speeches, music, and a pageant with people dressed as the French, Spanish, English, and Native Americans displaying large flags. The show was a huge success. "The carving of Rushmore is not a thing of today but of the ages. . . . It is the most stupendous undertaking of its kind in all history," gushed one newspaper.

Two years passed before work could begin on the actual carving. During that time Borglum worked on his plans, examining the mountain carefully to see where and how to carve, then sketching and making models of proposed designs. By now he had settled on

presidential portraits on an epic scale. Washington, Jefferson, and Lincoln were obvious choices. As first president, George Washington was the father of his country. Thomas Jefferson, the third president, had written most of the Declaration of Independence in 1776, and while president, began the expansion west with his purchase of the Louisiana Territory. Abraham Lincoln, the sixteenth president, guided the nation through its most terrible era, the Civil War. He had preserved the Union.

Borglum's fourth selection of Theodore Roosevelt was more controversial. He had been the twenty-sixth president and had died in 1919. There were many who would have preferred Woodrow Wilson, twenty-eighth president, who led the country through the First World War. He had died only a year before in 1924. There was also a grassroots campaign to include Susan B. Anthony, the great campaigner for the equality of women. But Borglum was adamant. Both he and Senator Norbeck were admirers of Roosevelt, who had focused the nation's attention on the conservation of our natural wonders, and who had built the Panama Canal, greatly expanding America's influence in the world. In the end Borglum simply made his decision: to include Roosevelt and ignore his critics.

Beyond artistic questions, the engineering problems encountered in carving a mountain are formidable, and Borglum had to figure out just how to proceed. Equipment had to be assembled, the business arrangements had to be worked out, and most importantly, money had to be raised.

THE CARVING OF MOUNT RUSHMORE COST EXACTLY $989,992.32. Of this, about $154,000 was raised privately, through donations and promotional efforts. By far the greatest portion, $836,000 was funded by Congress. Borglum was paid a total of $170,000. In the end, Mount Rushmore was financed mainly by the federal government, but for the first ten years of work money was a constant problem, and raising it a constant challenge. Proud of his business and social contacts, Borglum bragged that he could produce wealthy donors eager to spend their money on his project, but this turned out to be mainly wishful thinking. The good people of South Dakota, while generally supportive, were not inclined to contribute much of their hard-earned money to carve a mountain, so it fell to Senator Norbeck and his colleague, Congressman William Williamson, to serve as the champions of Mount Rushmore in Washington, and to get the legislation passed to fund it.

In the early 1930s, the nation entered a period of great economic hardship. The boom years of the twenties ended abruptly with the crash of the stock market in 1929. Suddenly the wealth held in banks and investments was practically worthless. During the Great Depression that followed, millions of people were out of work, and money was scarce. There were many critics who considered carving a mountain a foolish waste of money, but Senator Norbeck pointed out that Mount Rushmore provided jobs and in fact contributed to the South Dakota economy. Gradually the monument came to be seen as a great public works project, and more and more funding was approved. But the money came only bit by bit, and whenever money ran out, the work stopped. Of the fourteen years it took to complete Mount Rushmore, only about six and one-half years were spent actually carving. This was especially annoying to Borglum, who was impatient for his great work to proceed. Notoriously casual about money, Borglum thought about it only when it wasn't available. Otherwise, he felt entitled to spend it freely. This frequently caused problems with his sponsors.

In 1929, control of the business side of the project was placed in the hands of the Mount Rushmore National Memorial Commission. Its most important member was John A. Boland, a local South Dakota businessman who took on the responsibility for the Mount Rushmore finances. He had to pay the bills, keep an accounting of the funds, and deal with the temperamental Borglum, who could be petty and scheming when he didn't get his way. Borglum came to resent what he considered interference from Boland, but there is no doubt that the frugal businessman kept the project afloat during the hard times of the Great Depression. Therefore, John Boland can be considered one of the fathers of the Mount Rushmore National Memorial, along with Doane Robinson, Senator Peter Norbeck, Congressman William Williamson, and of course, Gutzon Borglum.

IN 1927, MOUNT RUSHMORE FIRST CAME to the general attention of the American people. President Calvin Coolidge chose South Dakota for his vacation and summer residence that year, and Gutzon Borglum persuaded him to speak at another dedication ceremony. On

August 10, 1927, all eyes were focused on Mount Rushmore, and Borglum, the master showman, did not disappoint.

The ceremony included a twenty-one gun salute produced by blasting tree stumps for the new road under construction. After some eloquent remarks from Coolidge, Borglum climbed the mountain and was lowered over the side of the cliff. Dangling there, he drilled several holes to the amazement of the crowd, which for the first time realized the scale of the monument. Two months later, on October 4, the first crew of workmen began attacking the granite with their drills. The carving of Mount Rushmore had begun.

ALTHOUGH GUTZON BORGLUM WAS THE SCULPTOR, he did not carve the mountain himself. He designed the monument and directed a crew of men who did the work. Their tools were dynamite and air-driven rock drills, or jackhammers.

In the months before carving began, carpenters worked at the base of the mountain building a studio for Borglum and quarters for the crew. Buildings were constructed for housing the pumps which supplied the compressed air for the jackhammers, and a workshop was built for the blacksmith, whose main responsibility was the continual sharpening of drill bits, which were quickly dulled by the granite. An aerial cable tram was installed to the mountaintop. It was very small, able to hold only three or four people, and was meant for hauling equipment. A wooden stairway was built for the crew. Going to

work each morning started with a forty-story climb of 506 steps, interrupted at intervals by forty-five platforms and ramps. On the summit, a cluster of structures rose — stairs, catwalks, platforms, and buildings. Hand winches were installed for raising and lowering specially designed sling seats suspended from cables. Pipe was laid to carry the compressed air to the jackhammers, and to power it all, a generating plant was built in Keystone, the nearest town.

Borglum's first task was to figure out a way to transfer his design ideas to the bulk of the mountain. At Stone Mountain, he had projected an image onto the rock with a projector that he himself invented. Following the projection, lines were painted to guide the carving. Then the relatively shallow relief carving made a picture on the smooth flank of Stone Mountain, like the images on a coin. But Mount Rushmore was too rugged for projection, and these carved faces would be sculpted almost fully in the round, like the faces of free-standing statues. Another method had to be used. After months of sketching and modeling in clay, Borglum prepared large working models of plaster. The proportions of these models were transferred to the mountain by a method called "pointing," a mechanical process used since ancient times for copying statues from smaller models.

The model was equipped with a horizontal measuring rod thirty inches long, attached at one end to the center of the top of the head. It could be rotated to any position, and from any point on the rod, a weighted tape could be hung straight down to measure any point on the model. For each head at Rushmore, a giant version of the pointing device was installed on top of the mountain, with a horizontal boom thirty *feet* long. This way, one inch on the model equalled one foot on the mountain. By establishing a center line on both model and mountain and coordinating the position of both pointing devices, any point on the surface of the model could be precisely measured, accurately enlarged, and its exact relative position located within the rock. By constantly pointing, the crew knew where and how much rock to remove.

Most of it was blasted away. Afraid of cracking the rock, Borglum was reluctant at first, but he was forced to use dynamite by the sheer scale of the job. With practice and by using very small charges carefully packed with sand into drill holes in the rock, the Rushmore crew learned to use the dynamite with great precision to remove vast amounts of stone and to rough in each face. In some places they blasted to within inches of the finished surface.

Borglum decided to get each head well started before beginning the next, so that he could continue to make adjustments in the overall scheme. The figure of George Washington was the first to be started, and his head was positioned to occupy the most prominent spot in the cliff.

Work proceeded slowly, whenever money became available, and as the rock was drilled and blasted away layer by layer, the features of the first president gradually emerged

from the granite. After the general shape of the face was roughed in, blasting gave way to *honeycombing*: Closely spaced holes were drilled to a specific shallow depth, determined by pointing. The rock left between the holes was chipped and chiseled away, sometimes in large slabs resembling honeycombs. The process could then be repeated, taking the rock down to the level of the final surface. At this stage Borglum could order minute adjustments, and the details were refined, giving the faces individuality and life. Finally, in a finishing process called *bumping*, the rough places and drill marks were ground away with a special drill bit.

Much like an architect, once his design was planned Borglum did not always have to be physically present for work to proceed. In the beginning the day-to-day work was supervised by Jesse G. Tucker, who had assisted at Stone Mountain, but the men who actually carved Rushmore were the local workmen who simply needed a job during the Great Depression of the 1930s — men like Red Anderson, Hoot Leach, Ray Grover, and Merle Peterson. The work was hard and dangerous, but the pay was quite good (by 1937 a carver was paid $1.25 an hour, a handsome wage in those days). Many of them had been miners, so they were familiar with blasting and drilling rock, but here they had to learn to handle their eighty-five pound jackhammers while dangling from a windswept cliff — "hanging out there on that dinky cable," as one workman said. In summer they sweltered from the heat radiating from the sun-baked rock, and in winter they worked behind tarpaulins stretched over scaffolds lowered from the mountaintop, until bitter cold forced them to stop. On days of severe weather, the crew would play cards and complain, for they were paid only when they worked. And whenever the money ran out they had to go find other jobs until Rushmore started up again.

They were a rough and ready bunch that worked hard and played hard, and for many of them, weekends offered the chance to blow off steam after a week of labor on the mountain. The younger, more footloose men drank and brawled at local honky-tonks on Saturday nights. "I guess you could say fighting at dances was sort of a hobby with us," one said. On Sundays they organized baseball games, eventually sending a team to the state championships. But then early on Monday mornings, they had to be ready to face the 506 steps to the mountaintop.

Considering the danger involved, it seems remarkable that no one was killed or even very badly injured while working on the mountain, although there were some close calls, several broken bones, and plenty of scrapes and scratches. Once the brake on the tram gave way. It hurled to the base of the mountain and a few men were hurt. On another occasion a lightning storm caused some dynamite to explode, startling the men who were dangling on the side of the cliff. But the greatest hazard from working on Rushmore was the granite dust. Several of the men who breathed it in day after day developed in later years a fatal lung disease called silicosis.

Moody and temperamental, Gutzon Borglum could be a hard boss, but over the years the crew developed a genuine affection for the "Old Man." For many of these men, Mount Rushmore became more than a job. Their pride and satisfaction grew as they began to see the results of their work. As Red Anderson expressed it, "At first, Rushmore was just another job and a crazy kind of job at that. It was just a place to earn some money and nothing more. . . . But the longer we were there, the more we began to sense that we were building a truly great thing, and after a while all of us old hands became truly dedicated to it." As much as anything, Mount Rushmore is a monument to the hard work of these men.

A DEDICATION FOR THE WASHINGTON HEAD WAS HELD JULY 4, 1930. By now the facial features were recognizable; in addition, in the position now occupied by Lincoln's forehead, the year 1776 was carved in letters about fifteen feet high. This was the beginning of what was to have been an elaborate inscription that Borglum called the Entablature. It was to be nothing less than a condensed history of the United States. Borglum asked President Calvin Coolidge to write it and he accepted. A great controversy arose when Borglum insulted Coolidge by changing his words. The title "1776" was blasted away when the Lincoln head was started, and the Entablature was never carved. Besides the inscription, Borglum's grandiose design included a monumental staircase and the Hall of Records, a kind of

museum and vault for the important documents and records of American history, to be hollowed out of the mountain itself, behind the faces.

Sometimes Borglum was forced to change his plans. In June 1931, as work continued on Washington, blasting began for Thomas Jefferson, but not the face we see today. In the original design, Jefferson was on Washington's right-hand side, not his left. As work progressed and more of the rock was removed, the stone underneath was revealed to be faulty and unsuitable for carving. It must have been an agonizing decision for Borglum to change his design so radically, but he had no choice but to blast away the original Jefferson in 1934, and start again on the other side of Washington. But even the new Jefferson gave Borglum some problems. This part of the granite contained veins of quartz, which were potential cracks. Borglum said that he had no intention of making a statue which might be missing a nose in a few hundred years, so he had to keep shifting the head's position as he blasted, until he found the best part of the rock. Even then, Jefferson's lip required a granite plug to patch a defect in the stone.

In 1936, blasting began on the Lincoln face, Washington's chest was roughed in, and Jefferson's face was finished enough for a dedication held on August 30. The guest of honor was the president of the United States, Franklin D. Roosevelt, who was fascinated by the model for the face of Theodore Roosevelt, his own cousin. After viewing the monument, even in its unfinished state, President Roosevelt declared, "I had seen the

photographs, I had seen the drawings, and I had talked with those who are responsible for this great work, and yet I had no conception, until about ten minutes ago, not only of its magnitude, but also of its permanent beauty and importance."

Work was progressing rapidly by the late 1930s. Mount Rushmore was now adequately funded by Congress, and the crew had become expert at carving mountains. In 1937 the Lincoln face was far enough along for a dedication ceremony, and Theodore Roosevelt was roughed in. Like Jefferson, Roosevelt was difficult to position because of faulty rock. Borglum had to keep blasting farther and farther back into the cliff, until he finally reached stone of the right quality. So much granite was removed that Roosevelt is carved on a relatively thin slab of rock only thirty feet thick.

By now Mount Rushmore was attracting many tourists. The problem of its remoteness had been solved by the opening of the Iron Mountain Road in 1933. This scenic route to Rushmore was planned personally by Senator Peter Norbeck, and getting it made was one of his great contributions to the project. The road goes through three tunnels. As you emerge from each, Mount Rushmore is framed by the arch of rock. Unfortunately, Senator Norbeck did not live to see the completion of the monument to which he had contributed so much; he died of cancer in 1936.

The late 1930s also saw some reorganization at Rushmore. Administrative control passed to the National Park Service, and Borglum was given authority over the entire carving operation. He no longer had to report to John Boland. In 1938, Lincoln Borglum, the sculptor's son, assumed responsibility for the day-to-day work. Now twenty-five years old, the new superintendent had accompanied his father on his very first trip to South Dakota in 1924, at the age of eleven. He had been intimate with the project from the beginning, starting at Rushmore as an unpaid helper and gradually working his way up to the position of pointer. Respected by the crew and trusted by his father, Lincoln had inherited some artistic sensitivity. He was the very best choice to take charge of transferring his father's vision to the mountain.

Work also began in 1938 on the excavation of the great room in the mountain for Borglum's Hall of Records. He felt it to be a very important part of the memorial, a kind of time capsule of the important artifacts of American culture so that future generations would know about the civilization that made this gigantic monument. When work stopped in 1941, a cave-like room about seventy-five feet deep had been roughed out, but the Hall was never finished, and in truth, Borglum was always rather vague about exactly what it would contain.

There would be one more dedication. The unveiling of the Roosevelt head was held in 1939. For the next two years, the crew continued their pointing, honeycombing, and bumping. There was only one major interruption. On March 6, 1941, three weeks after a surgical procedure, Gutzon Borglum died in Chicago of a heart attack. Vigorous almost

until the end, he was seventy-four years old at his death, although he had claimed to be only sixty-nine. The colorful artist, with his colossal vision of an inspiring and patriotic work of art, had lived to see his great masterpiece almost realized. He died one week after learning that there would be no more money for Mount Rushmore. Europe was at war and the money was needed to arm America, since many thought that the United States would be forced to enter the conflict.

The figures would never be carved to the waist as planned. After his father's death, Lincoln Borglum finished off work on the faces, using up the money that was left. October 31, 1941, was the last day of work on the mountain. Thirty-seven days later, on December 7, the Japanese bombed Pearl Harbor, and the United States entered World War II.

◆ ◆ ◆

At his own request, Gutzon Borglum's name is not carved on the mountain, but this is the only thing modest about his achievement. The four faces on Mount Rushmore are simply immense. Each measures about sixty feet from the top of the forehead to the chin. If the heads belonged to living men, they would be able to look into the upper floors of forty-five-story buildings and wade across great rivers. To carve them, 450,000 tons of rock were blasted and drilled away, forming a great pile at the base of the cliff. The finely finished surface of the sculpture covers twelve thousand square feet. Mount Rushmore is gigantic, but it is also beautiful. With dynamite and jackhammers, Borglum's crew turned his ideas into a work of art, for the four portraits are full of sensitivity, strength, idealism, and intelligence. Thanks to Borglum's skill as a sculptor, the eyes are alive and seem to look back at us. Many people are profoundly moved when they visit Mount Rushmore, and few images have become more familiar and beloved than these four faces carved on a mountain.

There have always been detractors. Some believed that it was arrogant for men to carve into mountains. Others objected to the expense. Native Americans have argued that the carvings desecrate sacred ground which was stolen from them. Lovers of more modern art have criticized the realistic style of the monument.

Over the years there have been many proposals to add more faces to Mount Rushmore. Democrats have championed Franklin D. Roosevelt and Republicans have proposed Ronald Reagan. But aside from plans to finish the incomplete Hall of Records as a more modest time capsule explaining the monument to future generations, it is very unlikely that Mount Rushmore will ever be changed in any significant way.

What has changed is the complex of buildings built on Doane Mountain across the valley for viewing the memorial. Over the decades more and more people have visited Mount Rushmore, until today, nearly three million people come every year. In the late 1990s, Mount Rushmore was provided with a new museum, visitors center, shop, hiking trail, and amphitheater, where visitors may observe a nightly lighting ceremony.

But Mount Rushmore National Memorial is far more than a tourist attraction. Planned in an era of national prosperity, built during a time of economic hardship, and finished on the eve of one of history's most terrible wars, it is a symbol of American optimism and a tribute to the power of the individual in a free society. Borglum's "Shrine of Democracy" has become one of the most familiar and inspiring of American patriotic landmarks, and it will endure for a very long time. Though the monument will gradually weather and erode, it should last tens of thousands of years. In the far distant future, barring catastrophe, the four faces will still speak to people for whom twentieth century America is ancient, remote, and strange, as a monument to all of humanity. Mount Rushmore is for the ages.

◆ ◆ ◆

TIME LINE

1924   Gutzon Borglum first visits the Black Hills

1925   Borglum chooses Mount Rushmore as a site

          Dedication ceremony — October 1

1926   Borglum begins planning the memorial

          Efforts are made to begin raising money

1927   Contracts are signed

          President Calvin Coolidge speaks at Rushmore — August 10

          Drilling begins — October 4

1928   Money runs out and work stops

1929   Congress begins funding Mount Rushmore

          Mount Rushmore National Memorial Commission first meets

1930   Dedication of George Washington

1931   Work continues

1932   Money runs out and work stops

1933   Mount Rushmore comes under the control of the
            National Park Service

1934   Thomas Jefferson is moved to the present location

1935   Work continues

1936   President Franklin Roosevelt attends the dedication of
            Thomas Jefferson — August 30

1937   Dedication of Abraham Lincoln

1938   Borglum is given complete control and Lincoln Borglum
            is made Superintendent

1939   Dedication of Theodore Roosevelt

1940   Work continues

1941   Gutzon Borglum dies — March 6

          Work stops on the mountain — October 31

BIBLIOGRAPHY

Dean, Robert J. *Living Granite: The Story of Borglum and The Mount Rushmore Memorial.* New York: Viking Press, 1949.

Fite, Gilbert C. *Mount Rushmore.* Norman: University of Oklahoma Press, 1952.

Prolman, Marilyn. *The Story of Mount Rushmore.* Chicago: Children's Press, 1969.

Smith, Rex Alan. *The Carving of Mount Rushmore.* New York: Abbeville Press, 1985.

All of my quotations come from Fite and Smith, and indeed, I am indebted to these two sources for most of my information. Both are well written, thoroughly researched, and very complete. Both tell the entire Rushmore story, but from the perspectives of two different generations.

Library of Congress Cataloging-in-Publication Data
Curlee, Lynn. Rushmore / Lynn Curlee. — 1st ed.   p.   cm.
Summary: Describes how this patriotic shrine and tourist attraction was conceived, designed, and created by the dedicated artist Gutzon Borglum.
ISBN 0-590-22573-1
1. Borglum, Gutzon, 1867-1941 — Juvenile literature. 2. Mount Rushmore National Memorial (S.D.) — Juvenile literature. [1. Mount Rushmore National Memorial (S.D.)
2. National monuments. 3. Borglum, Gutzon, 1867-1941.] I. Title. NB237.B6C86   1998   730'.92 — dc21   98-16891   CIP   AC

The text type is set in Garamond 3. • Book design by Nancy Sabato
The illustrations are acrylic paintings reproduced in full color from photographic transparencies.
Mr. Curlee wishes to thank Ed Peterson for photographing the paintings.

10 9 8 7 6 5 4 3   0/0 01 02 03
Printed in Mexico   49
FIRST EDITION, APRIL 1999

◆ ◆ ◆